This igloo book
belongs to:

....

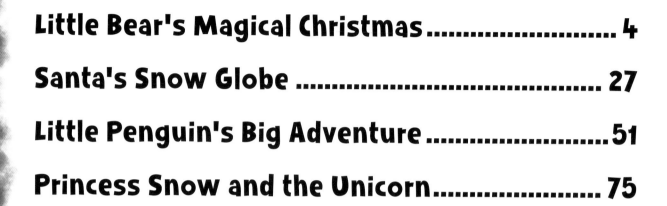

igloobooks

Published in 2019
by Igloo Books Ltd
Cottage Farm
Sywell
NN6 0BJ
www.igloobooks.com

0719 001.01
2 4 6 8 10 9 7 5 3 1
ISBN 978-1-83852-016-8

Little Bear's Magical Christmas written by Melanie Joyce and illustrated by Gabi Murphy
Santa's Snow Globe written by Stephanie Moss and illustrated by Ned Taylor
Little Penguin's Big Adventure written by Melanie Joyce and illustrated by Gareth Llewhellin & Dave Williams
Princess Snow and the Unicorn written by Melanie Joyce and illustrated by Jenny Wren

Designed by Alex Alexandrou
Edited by Stephanie Moss

Printed and manufactured in China

My First
Christmas
Treasury

igloobooks

One Christmas, Little Bear said, "I'm not writing to Santa this year.
There's no point sending a letter, because Santa won't be here."

"Why won't Santa come?" asked his curious mum and dad.
"Well you see," said Little Bear, "I've been a little bit bad."

5

"I went to the kitchen cupboard and dipped my paw in the honey.
Oh, but it was so delicious, so **dribbly** and **sticky** and **runny**."

6

"Then I didn't tidy my room when Mummy told me to."

"Don't worry about that," said Mummy Bear.
"I'm not cross with you."

7

"Oh, but there's more,"
said Little Bear.
"Quite a bit more than that."

"When Aunty came to stay,
I tried on her **fancy** new hat."

"I took it outside, when I shouldn't have,
because I wanted to play."

"All of a sudden
a big **gust** of wind

whooshed

and blew it away."

Little Bear told his mum and dad about when he'd made too much noise.

And when his friends came over, he had refused to share his toys.

"So, you see," said Little Bear, "why I can't write to Santa Claus."
He looked sadly at the Christmas tree and **twiddled** his furry paws.

"Oh, Bear," said Daddy kindly, "you're forgetting the good things you've done."

"Like when you made Aunty giggle, and she had lots of fun."

"And remember when you gave your friends your tin of **yummy** treats? You shared them out at the picnic, so everyone had some sweets."

"Santa won't think you're bad," said Mummy, "because you made mistakes. He'll remember **special** times like when you made Daddy cupcakes."

Suddenly Little Bear's happiness all came **flooding** back.
"Go and write Santa that letter," said Mummy, "and I'll make you a snack."

So Little Bear wrote a letter and posted it that day.
An elf took it to Santa, at the North Pole far away.

"I wonder if Santa got my letter," said Little Bear on Christmas Eve.
"Magic things happen at Christmas," said Mummy. "You just need to believe."

Little Bear tried to stay awake, but soon slept quiet as a mouse.
It was then that Santa and his reindeer **flew** right over his house.

With a **jingle** of bells, Santa left presents under the Christmas tree.
He wrote a special note for Little Bear to see.

"Ho, ho, ho," said Santa, as he flew off into the air.
"There'll be smiles tomorrow morning for one happy little bear."

On Christmas morning Little Bear **bounded** out of bed.

Under the tree were presents.
"Santa's been," he said.

Santa's note said,

"Dear Little Bear,
I've left you some presents here.
Thank you for being so good.
I'll see you again next year."

Little Bear was **overjoyed** that Santa had come to call.
It was going to be a very merry Christmas after all.

Santa's
Snow Globe

Everyone in the North Pole had finished work for Christmas,
except for Santa. Mrs Claus sipped hot cocoa, as the elves
sledged down snowy hills. **"Ho-ho-ho!"** called Santa,
who was excited to start his deliveries.

Santa carried one last present to the sleigh, as the reindeer munched on crunchy carrots. Suddenly, he tripped and dropped the heavy gift on his big toe. **"Owww!"** cried Santa, clutching his sore foot and hopping around in the snow.

Santa tried everything he could think of to make his toe stop hurting. First, he put a bag of frozen peas on it. Then, he dipped it in the icy lake.

"Maybe if I put on Mrs Claus' special fluffy slippers," hoped Santa, **"my toe won't hurt so much,"** but it was no use. It didn't feel any better!

"There's only one thing for it," said Mrs Claus. "We'll have to call the Elf Doctor." Suddenly, he appeared, with a twinkle and a flash.
"I'm afraid you must rest your foot tonight," said the Elf Doctor, peering at Santa's big, red toe and shaking his head. "Do not leave the North Pole!"

"Maybe I can go and deliver all the presents, instead," thought Mrs Claus.

So, she jumped into the sleigh and whistled to some of the elves for help.

She pulled on the reins, but to her surprise, the reindeer didn't move!

Meanwhile, Santa called his friend, the magic Christmas Fairy.

"How will the presents be delivered now that I can't do it?" he asked her.

Just then, the Christmas Fairy appeared with a special gift and said,

"Here, this snow globe is magical. It will help you save Christmas!"

At that moment, Mrs Claus burst in. **"We tried to deliver the presents for you ourselves,"** she cried, **"but the reindeer wouldn't take off!"** **"Thank you,"** said Santa, chuckling, **"but the reindeer need their magical flying dust."** Then, he gave her a special key to unlock the dust store.

34

Santa began telling them everything they would need to know to do his work for him. **"Here, take these headsets so we can talk to each other,"** said Santa, **"but I'll need to see you to really be able to help."** Then, Santa remembered the magical snow globe. He shook it and saw the sleigh inside.

So, Mrs Claus sprinkled the reindeer with magical dust and they took off into the sky. Sure enough, when Santa shook the snow globe, he saw the sleigh, flying safely above him. **"Where do we go first, Santa?"** asked Mrs Claus, speaking into her headset. He told her the special satnav code and they sped off on their way.

They hadn't gone far, when the reindeer began to feel a bit grumpy! **"Uh-oh,"** said Merry Elf. **"Santa, what should we do?"** Santa spoke over the headset, **"I always keep a secret stash of crunchy apples in the sleigh to cheer them up,"** he said.

Santa watched them in the globe and, before long, began to worry, as it was time for them to land the sleigh for the first time.

Mrs Claus had never driven a sleigh before, let alone landed one on a roof. **"Okay... you'll have to talk me through it,"** she said, feeling nervous.

Santa guided Mrs Claus, step by step, using the magical globe.
"Left a bit, right a bit. Now, pull on the reins!" he called.

With a skid and a bump, Mrs Claus landed the sleigh safely on the roof.
"Ouch!" said Glitter Elf, falling and landing on her bottom.

39

Inside the house, the elves felt puzzled. **"Which presents do we deliver?"** they asked. Santa looked in the globe and read from his list. Next, he told Sparkle Elf some special magic words so they wouldn't wake the sleeping dog!

Santa helped Mrs Claus and the elves deliver presents all
night long until, soon, they could do it all on their own.
He saw them travel the whole world, inside the snow globe.

42

In fact, Santa thought they'd all done such a good job of saving Christmas, he wanted to do something special to thank them. With a little help from the Christmas Fairy, he opened the window and called to his North Pole friends.

The Christmas Fairy got straight to work and, with a swish of her magic wand, the whole of the North Pole was decorated for a special party. She even made a glittering ice rink for everyone to skate on.

"Perfect," she said, with a twinkling smile.

44

Jolly Elf helped Freezy Snowman and Fluffy Bunny use the elves' workshop to make some last-minute thank you gifts.

Santa even hobbled to the kitchen and tried to bake some special treats for them, but he burned every last one. **"Oh dear,"** he said.

When Mrs Claus and the elves arrived back at the North Pole,
the snowmen, elves and bunnies all shouted, **"Surprise!"**
Everyone enjoyed the party, whizzing and twirling on the ice, but
Santa was the most excited of all to see Mrs Claus and the elves.

"Thank you for delivering the presents for me," he said, seeing the happy children in the snow globe on Christmas morning. **"We couldn't have done it without you,"** said Mrs Claus, **"and a little bit of Christmas magic, of course!"**

NORTH POLE

Little Penguin's Big Adventure

Little Penguin was bored with making friends out of snow.
"I'll just sit here and wait for something exciting to happen," he said.
So, Little Penguin waited and waited, but nothing happened at all.

Suddenly, a seagull swooped down. "You need to find Adventure," he said. "Where's Adventure?" asked the puzzled penguin. The seagull pointed to a small, red boat, bobbing on the sea. "I think it's that way," he replied.

SQUAWK!

On the small, red boat, Little Penguin asked the captain
a question. "Do you know the way to Adventure?"
The captain twiddled his bristles. "I think it's that way,"
he said, pointing to a distant desert island.

WHOOOO! went the wind, as the waves lapped and slapped at the small, red boat.

WHOOOO!
it went again, as the great sea swelled and rolled.
Soon, Little Penguin felt very, very sick.

Little Penguin hopped off the small, red boat at a desert island.
"Shiver me timbers!" cried a fierce pirate captain and his mad pirate crew,
who happened to be passing. "He's after our treasure!"

"I'm just trying to find Adventure," replied Little Penguin. "Can you show me the way, please?"

"Arrr, it be that way," said the pirate captain, swishing his cutlass to point at his ship.

On the pirate ship, there was a lot of swabbing the decks, eating ship's biscuits and sailing the Seven Seas. "But where is Adventure?" asked Little Penguin. "It be that way," said the crafty captain, pointing to a plank that poked out to sea.

Little Penguin walked along the plank until...

...SPLASH!

Down, down he went,
to the bottom of the sea,
but he wasn't alone.

"Hellooo," said a shark, with his best sharky smile.

"Err, do you know the way to Adventure?" asked Little Penguin, nervously.

"Go that way," replied the shark. "But you had better be quick!"

SNAP, SNAP, SNAP!

Little Penguin swam as fast as he could.
He darted and dashed under the coral, over the reef,
behind the rocks and **WHOOSH!** out of the sea...

... **WHEE!** into a tree. Oo-oo! went some cheeky monkeys swinging by.

"Do you know where I can find Adventure?" asked Little Penguin.

"Oh, yes," replied the naughty monkeys, **OO-OO-OOING** and making a racket. "It's that way," they said, pointing to the bush.

The bush was quiet, there was hardly a sound. Only the leaves rustled and the parrots squawked and it was very, very still until...

... **ROAR!** went the lion who was hiding there.

Little Penguin ran and ran as fast as he could, through the trees, by the waterhole and down the hill.

There were **HISSES** and **SNAPS** and **SNORTS** and **SQUAWKS!**

"Which way to Adventure?" cried Little Penguin, as he sped past the flamingos. "I think it's that way," said the flamingo leader, pointing to a sailing boat.

Little Penguin jumped into the boat and sailed off down the river. The river grew wider and became the ocean and before too long, a great storm blew.

Poor Little Penguin was all alone.

"I don't want to find Adventure any more!" cried Little Penguin and he began to cry. He missed his mummy and daddy. He missed being bored and sitting on his rock and twiddling his flippers.
"I want to go home!" he sobbed.

Just then, a great whale sprayed seawater from his spout.

SWOOSH!

"Don't cry, Little Penguin," he said. "I know exactly
where home is," and he pointed to an iceberg far, far away.
So, Little Penguin jumped on his back and off they went.

At home, his mummy and daddy were waiting on the shore.
"Where have you been, Little Penguin?" they asked. "It's nearly bedtime."
Little Penguin told them all about the places he had been.
"It sounds like you found Adventure," said Dad.

SQUAWK! went the seagull and Little Penguin smiled.
"Yes, I think I did," he said. "But I don't want to go there again.
There's nothing better than being at home." With that,
Little Penguin snuggled down for a long and dreamy sleep.

Princess Snow
and the Unicorn

Long ago, in a kingdom of winter, there lived a princess called Snow. She loved her cold and frosty home, but Snow didn't have any friends and was very lonely.

One day, her mother, the ice queen, gave the sad princess
a beautiful snow globe. "Sometimes, all you need is a
little magic," said the queen with a smile.

Snow looked into the globe. There were ice maidens and fairies.
There were snowmen and a princess with a golden tiara,
riding a beautiful unicorn.

"I wish that was me," said Snow, shaking the globe so the snowflakes swirled and danced. Suddenly, the princess felt like she was swirling and spinning, down, down, until...

... Snow found herself in a magical world. Fairies fluttered around her and a shining unicorn shook his mane as tiny fairy bells tinkled. "I'm inside the globe," gasped Snow.

"Yes, Princess," said the unicorn, "because you wished it so."
The fairies fluttered around excitedly. "We'll be your friends!"
they cried, giggling.

The fairies lifted the princess onto the back of the unicorn.
Up, up they flew, over fields and hedges thick with snow, over
a sparkling palace to a frozen lake where snowmen stood.

"How sweet they are," said the princess. She touched their frosty noses
and the fairy bells jingled. One snowman blinked, then another.
"Hello, Princess," they said. "Come and dance with us."

Magical instruments played sweet music and the snowmen began to sway. They held Snow's hand and danced in a circle. With each step they moved faster and faster.

Round and round they flew, jigging and whirling
to the enchanting music.

The unicorn shook his mane and the fairy bells jingled.
The snowmen stood still as four beautiful ice maidens glided
across the lake. They bowed and gently took Snow's hand.

The princess twirled and danced as if she were a graceful ballerina,
elegantly holding her arms like the wings of a beautiful swan.

Once more, the unicorn shook his mane and Snow found herself on his back. "To the rainbow!" cried the fairies as they swooshed upwards. "Goodbye, snowmen. Goodbye, ice maidens," called Snow.

Far above the clouds arched a beautiful rainbow. The fairies collected icicles from the clouds and dipped them into the rainbow to make gems to decorate Snow's hair.

"How beautiful," said Snow, as the gems glittered in the sunlight.
"I wish I could show my mother." The unicorn shook his mane
and the magic bells tinkled. "As you wish, Princess," he said.

Suddenly, it began to snow. Thick flakes fell as the unicorn flew down, down. "Goodbye, Princess," said the faint voices of the fairies as they disappeared into the swirling curtain.

"Goodbye," said the unicorn, softly.
"Remember, we will always be your friends."
"Thank you," said Snow, as she watched the whirling
flakes spinning all around.

The princess felt like she was spinning too, down, down and far below, someone was calling her name. "Snow, Snow..."

"Snow, wake up," said the ice queen. Princess Snow gave
her mother the biggest hug, cuddling into her soft cape.
"The snow globe is amazing," she said.

"Yes, it's magic," said the queen, smiling as she helped the princess into her sleigh. Snow looked into the enchanted globe. "Now I will always have friends," she said, as the sleigh sped off across the glittering ice.